backstage pass

Just JUSTIN

Get With 'N SYNC's Total Babe!

By Kimberly Walsh
with Anne Raso

SCHOLASTIC INC.

New York   Toronto   London   Auckland   Sydney   Mexico City   New Delhi   Hong Kong

Photography Credits:

Front Cover: Ilpo Musto/London Features; Back Cover: Anthony Cutajar/London Features (top); Steve Granitz/Retna (bottom); Page 1: Bernhard Kuhmstedt/Retna; Page 3: Bernhard Kuhmstedt/Retna; Page 4: Bernhard Kuhmstedt/Retna; Page 5: Retna (top); Bernhard Kuhmstedt/Retna (bottom); Page 6: Pierre ZonZon/South Beach Photo Agency (left); Joseph Galea (right); Page 7: Bernhard Kuhmstedt/Retna; Page 8: Patrick G. Falcone/South Beach Photo Agency; Page 9: Bernhard Kuhmstedt/Retna (left); Bernhard Kuhmstedt/Retna (right); Page 10: Bernhard Kuhmstedt/Retna; Page 11: Steve Granitz/Retna (bottom); Page 12: Melanie Edwards/Retna (top); Tom Zuback/Retna (bottom); Page 13: Bernhard Kuhmstedt/Retna; Page 14: Steve Granitz/Retna (top); Jon Super/Retna (bottom); Page 15: Steve Granitz/Retna (top); Bernhard Kuhmstedt/Retna (bottom); Page 16: Ron Wolfson/London Features; Page 17: Bernhard Kuhmstedt/Retna (top); Bernhard Kuhmstedt/Retna (bottom); Page 18: Dennis Van Tine/London Features; Page 19: George De Sota/London Features (top); Jeff Slocomb/Corbis Outline (bottom); Page 20: Anthony Cutajar/London Features; Page 21: George De Sota/London Features (top); Gary Gershoff/Retna (bottom); Page 22: Bernhard Kuhmstedt/Retna (top); Bernhard Kuhmstedt/Retna (bottom); Page 23: Jeff Slocomb/Corbis Outline (top); Pages 24-25: Bernhard Kuhmstedt/Retna; page 26: John James/London Features (top); Bernhard Kuhmstedt/Retna (bottom); Page 27: Janet Macoska; Page 28: Steve Granitz/Retna; Armando Gallo/Retna (inset); Page 29: Bernhard Kuhmstedt/Retna (top); Anthony Cutajar/London Features (bottom); Page 30: Rodolphe Baras/London Features; Page 31: Melanie Edwards/Retna (top); Bernhard Kuhmstedt/Retna (bottom); Page 32: Bernhard Kuhmstedt/Retna (left); Thomas Lau/Corbis Outline (right); Page 33: Maggie Rodriguez/South Beach Photo Agency; Page 34: Pierre ZonZon/South Beach Photo Agency (top); Gregg DeGuire/London Features (bottom); Page 35: Bernhard Kuhmstedt/Retna; Page 36: Thomas Lau/Corbis Outline (top); Page 37: Melanie Edwards/Retna; page 38: Kelly A. Swift/Retna; Pages 38-39: South Beach Photo Agency; Page 39: Janet Macoska; Page 40: Bernhard Kuhmstedt/Retna (top); Steve Granitz/Retna (bottom); Page 42: Jen Lowery/London Features (top); Bernhard Kuhmstedt/Retna (bottom); Page 43: Melanie Edwards/Retna; Page 44: John James/London Features (top); Todd Kaplan/Star File (bottom left); James Sorensen/UPN (bottom right); Page 45: Paul Smith/Featureflash (middle); Chris Moody/Hutchins Photo Agency (bottom); Page 46: Steve Granitz/Retna; Page 48: Dennis Van Tine/London Features.

ISBN 0-439-17450-3

Design by Peter Koblish

Copyright © 2000 Scholastic Inc. All rights reserved. Published by Scholastic Inc. SCHOLASTIC and associated logos are trademarks and/or registered trademarks of Scholastic Inc.

12 11 10 9 8 7 6 5 4   0 1 2 3 4 5 6/0

Printed in the U.S.A.
First Scholastic printing, January 2000

GUIDE TO WHAT'S INSIDE

Justin "grandstands" with a handstand.

INTRODUCTION

And the winner is . . . *JUSTIN TIMBERLAKE!*

Justin

That joyful announcement came via *Teen People* magazine, and the results of its poll — which aired nationally on ABC-TV — asking fans to name the 21 Hottest Stars under the age of 21. Hyper-famous folk like Nick Carter, Britney, Brandy, James Van Der Beek, Usher, and Lance Bass were all on the list — but when it came to who got the most votes, a certain curly-haired cutie took top honors.

Justin Timberlake, of the band 'N Sync, winning a whopping thirty percent of the on-line vote, stepped into that spotlight all by himself.

His reaction was typically humble. Although he acknowledged his win — "There's no better feeling than having this much support," he told the magazine's readers — he knows that even though he may have been singled out, he hardly got to the top on

The "baby" of the group is the bounciest, too—JC, Lance, Joey, and Chris watch Justin take a trampoline tumble.

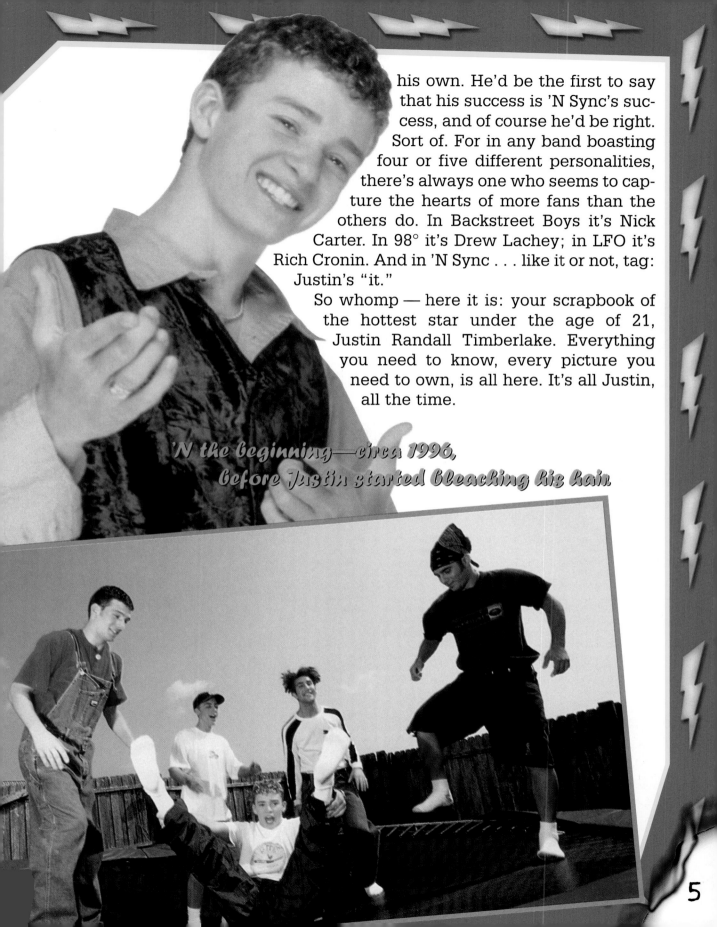

his own. He'd be the first to say that his success is 'N Sync's success, and of course he'd be right. Sort of. For in any band boasting four or five different personalities, there's always one who seems to capture the hearts of more fans than the others do. In Backstreet Boys it's Nick Carter. In 98° it's Drew Lachey; in LFO it's Rich Cronin. And in 'N Sync . . . like it or not, tag: Justin's "it."

So whomp — here it is: your scrapbook of the hottest star under the age of 21, Justin Randall Timberlake. Everything you need to know, every picture you need to own, is all here. It's all Justin, all the time.

'N the beginning—circa 1996, before Justin started bleaching his hair

5

CHAPTER ONE
JUST a Little Boy With a Big Talent

"If I could talk, I could sing. I was always performing for somebody." That's Justin's easy-does-it explanation for how he got so far, so fast. His uncle agrees: "Whether he was telling a joke, or dancing in front of everybody at Christmas, Justin was always the entertainer." It's what he always did. It just came naturally.

So did his desire to become a professional entertainer. Aside from a fleeting ambition to become the next Michael Jordan-like basketball star, Justin never really wanted to do anything else besides sing and dance in front of an audience. As a little kid, he'd sing all the time. He could hear a song on the radio and have it down in a minute. He loved listening to the harmonies of groups like Boyz II Men and the heartfelt funk of Stevie Wonder. He'd watch MTV as much as he could, too — imitating some of those videos is how he first learned to dance.

Still, little Justin might not have taken the leap into the professional spotlight had it not

Justin's on the cell phone, 24/7

To make sure his voice is always in shape, Justin works with a vocal coach.

6

been for a family split. When he was only seven years old, his parents, Lynn and Randall Timberlake, began divorce proceedings. The rupture was hard on him, as it might be on any kid, but there *was* a silver lining. Justin — an only child at the time — and his mom moved away from their hometown of Memphis, Tennessee, and resettled in Orlando, Florida. That's where Justin's performing career got a kick start. From the get go, the little boy entered contests — the first one he nabbed top prize in was called, "Dance Like the New Kids on the Block." It was 1989, when that group was in its heyday, sold millions of records, and won the hearts of fans the world over. Little could the dancing dervish know that less than a decade later, *he'd* be part of a group every bit as popular.

He did, however, do the prep work. Smart enough not to rely solely on his own natural talent, Justin took professional lessons — lots of 'em. He studied (and practiced!) piano and guitar, worked with a vocal coach, and took every possible opportunity to be in school plays or community talent shows, where he often nabbed the lead.

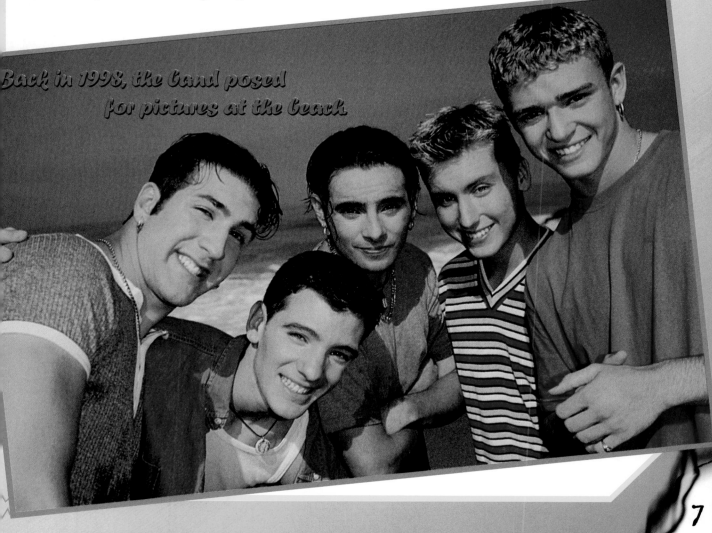

Back in 1998, the band posed for pictures at the beach

His favorite music? It changes daily, but *The Miseducation of Lauryn Hill* is what's on his CD player most.

At Disney World, Justin, with a little friend on his knee, played tourist on the tram.

The hard work, ambition, and obvious joy of performing first paid off in 1992. That's when Justin auditioned for and beat out 5000 other hopefuls to win a part in TV's *The New Mickey Mouse Club,* a variety/sketch show that aired on the Disney Channel. The show, nicknamed *MMC,* featured a revolving group of about 20 regulars — all teenagers — and had been on the air since 1989. When Justin rotated into it, he was only 12 years old, at that time the youngest cast member. "It

was a great opportunity. I was able to prepare myself as a singer and dancer," he says.

While a regular cast member, Justin reported for work each day at the Disney/MGM Studios at Disney World, and then attended school, where he carried a full junior high school workload. Naturally, he carried on a full social life as well, making close friends often and easily.

Joshua — JC — Chasez, an *MMC* cast member since 1991, became one of his best buddies. Not only did the guys get along personally, they also connected musically. Offstage, they'd compose original music, trade harmonies, even record demos, and dream about being part of a band.

It would be a few years before that dream came true. In 1994, *MMC* was abruptly canceled — and Justin had little choice but to leave his showbiz friends behind and return to Memphis with his mom. He also went back to public school. Being a "regular kid" did not agree with him. "I got so bored and down about everything," he confided in *Teen People,* "I started to get a little rebellious. I didn't really get into trouble, but I wasn't focusing like I could. I didn't have the inspiration that music gave me. That's my place in the world. That's where I belong."

Justin "got back" to where he belonged a scant year later. That's when he got a phone call that changed his life. "It was fate," he said.

'N FACT!

Real Full Name: Justin Randall Timberlake

Birthday: January 31, 1981

Hometown: Memphis, Tennessee

The 'Rents: Lynn and Paul Harless; Randy and Lisa Timberlake

Siblings: Half brothers Jonathan, 6, and Steven Timberlake, 1, who live with Justin's dad and stepmom in Tennessee.

Height: 5' 11"

Hair: Blond and famously curly. Most of his life, he's worn it short; only once, around age 14, did he try growing it below his ears. It proved too unruly.

Eyes: Blue

What's Justin's best feature? Hands down . . . according to him . . . it's his hands!

CHAPTER TWO
JUST Friends — the 'N Sync Connection

Fate came in the form of a dude named Chris Kirkpatrick, a talented singer/dancer who worked in Orlando. When he started to put a band together, one of the first people he recruited was fellow performer Joey Fatone.

Justin and JC didn't know it, but that connection would soon change their lives. For while not a regular cast member of *The New Mickey Mouse Club,* Joey happened to be one of the dancers who appeared in the opening and closing numbers of the show each week. Which made the easygoing dude a pal of Justin's and JC's. When

MMC was canceled, Joey and Chris wondered if JC and Justin would want to be part of their up 'n' coming band. They didn't have to wonder for long — both guys immediately agreed. Reeling in Louisiana native Lance Bass completed the quintet. Justin's mom thought up their name, and 'N Sync was born.

It's been five mad-crazy years for the boys, overflowing with nonstop rehearsing, recording, traveling, singing, dancing, doing interviews, photo sessions, and meeting fans. In that time, the band has endured its share of disappointments, but

Justin's got a few thoughts on the boys in the band. Listen in as he shares them.

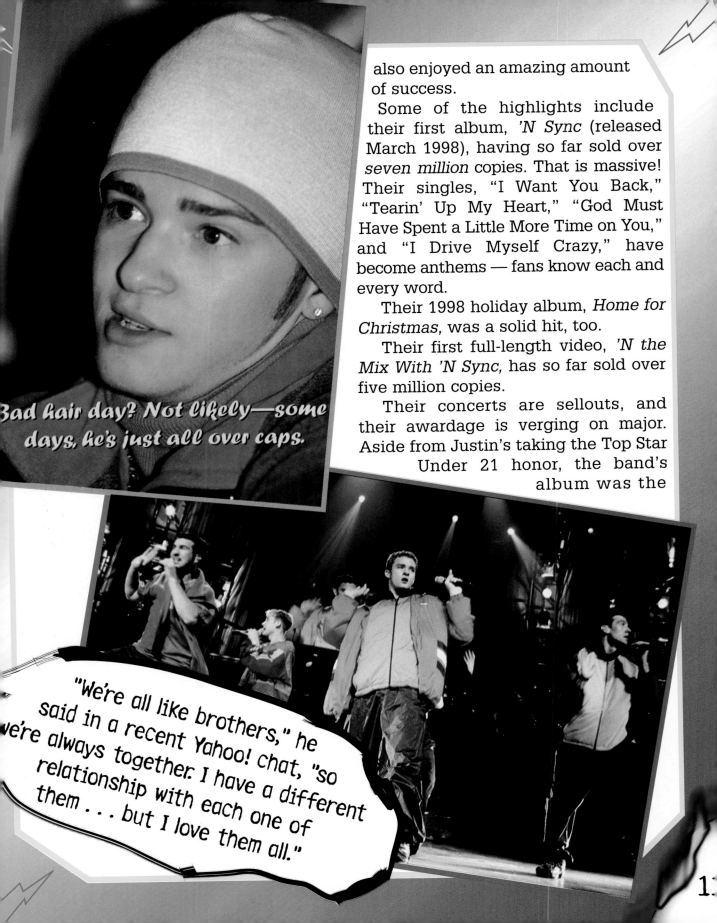

Bad hair day? Not likely—some days, he's just all over caps.

also enjoyed an amazing amount of success.

Some of the highlights include their first album, *'N Sync* (released March 1998), having so far sold over *seven million* copies. That is massive! Their singles, "I Want You Back," "Tearin' Up My Heart," "God Must Have Spent a Little More Time on You," and "I Drive Myself Crazy," have become anthems — fans know each and every word.

Their 1998 holiday album, *Home for Christmas,* was a solid hit, too.

Their first full-length video, *'N the Mix With 'N Sync,* has so far sold over five million copies.

Their concerts are sellouts, and their awardage is verging on major. Aside from Justin's taking the Top Star Under 21 honor, the band's album was the

"We're all like brothers," he said in a recent Yahoo! chat, "so we're always together. I have a different relationship with each one of them . . . but I love them all."

Teen Choice Album of the Year, and they copped an American Music Award as well. "That one was really phat," Justin gushed, "'cause we didn't expect it. We thought Third Eye Blind might win."

Maybe they should start expecting to clear more space on their mantels — 'N Sync is in a winning groove.

But . . . what about the personal stuff? Clearly, after all this time, the boys of 'N Sync know each other really, really well — better even than some of their family members. Here's Justin's take on his 'N Sync buddies — and theirs on him!

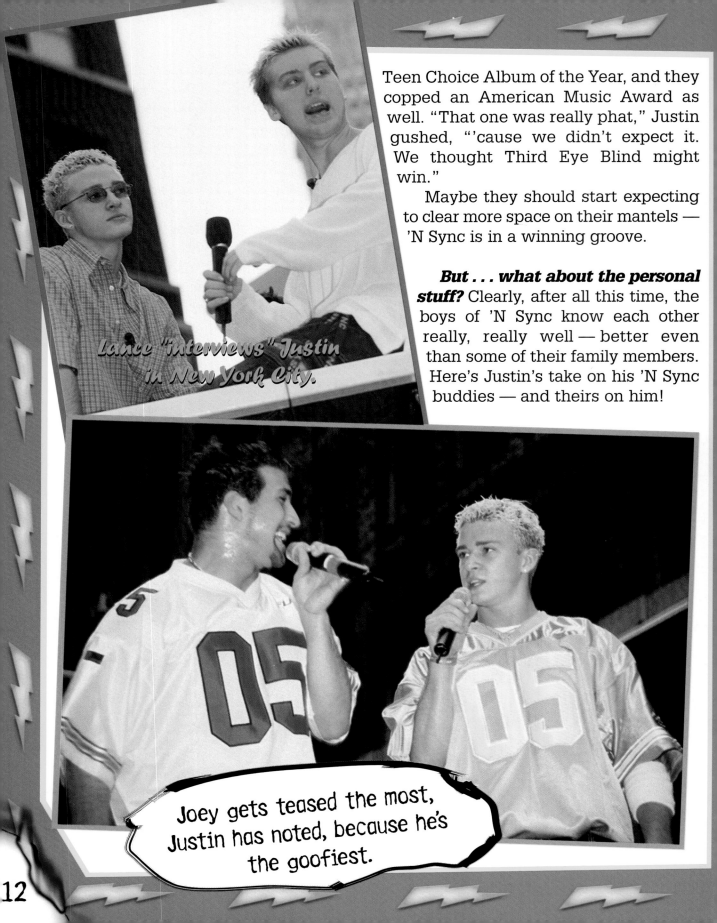

Lance "interviews" Justin in New York City.

Joey gets teased the most, Justin has noted, because he's the goofiest.

12

During an AOL chat, he dished: "Chris is really hyper — and I think it's funny when he gets that way." On Yahoo! he added, "Chris is the biggest prankster, and JC is the easiest one to pull a prank on. JC falls for everything.

"JC is quite serious and one of my pet peeves is that he always comes into a conversation in the middle and asks a question that was asked, like, five minutes ago. He does that every time!

"Joey is by far the biggest flirt. Whenever we argue about who gets to talk to a girl first, Joey always wins. But he gets picked on the most, too, 'cause he's the goofiest."

Since every good dish deserves another — turn the page to see what the guys posted about Justin in an Internet interview.

When 'N Sync is on the road—which is, pretty much, always—Justin does 300 push-ups a day in his hotel room. That's one way he stays buff.

Chris: "Justin is our youngest member, but he's also the most mature. He's got a really good head on his shoulders. When it's time to work, he's always there to work. He's very responsible and knows what's expected of him. That's really impressive, given his age."

Joey: "Justin is like our athletic dude! He always loves playing basketball. Whenever he has the time, he does a lot of working out. He does the working out for most of us! He's a sporty guy. Plus, he's always thinking ahead and trying to be successful."

There is, of course, the jealousy potential. It's no secret that Justin's the heartthrob, the one who gets the most fan mail, the loudest screams, the most coverage.

About *that,* 'N Sync 'n-sists — it's not an issue. Chris attributes it to Justin's age. "He's the one closest in age to the fans," he told *TV Guide.* "They think they have a chance to date him."

During an AOL chat, Justin himself avowed, "We don't pay attention to stuff like that. We have a lot of fun together, and we have a nice group vibe, so it's not important."

Of course, they argue sometimes — who wouldn't, spending so much time together in close quarters? "Sometimes we get on each other's nerves, but we don't get sick of each other," he reported in a recent on-line interview. "We get tired from being on the road. But we started off as friends, so even offstage, we like to hang out with each other."

Shiny, happy people 'cause they just won an American Music Award!

Justin tries not to eat a lot of chocolate, but his favorite ice cream is chocolate mocha chip.

Surf's up for 'N Sync, 'cause their album was voted the Teen Choice!

'N FACT!

Band Nickname: The guys have dubbed him Curly, The Baby, Mr. Smooth, and Bounce. The last has to do with his love for basketball.

Graduation Day: While a member of 'N Sync, Justin continued his high school studies — by mail. He took accredited correspondence courses and graduated — early — in 1998.

Award Boy: When 'N Sync accepted the Teen Choice Award for Album of the Year, Justin spoke on behalf of his bandmates. "I think . . . wow! . . . this is phat!" He then humbly added, "We thank God for giving us the opportunity to do what we love to do."

Fly Boy: During their concerts, 'N Sync does a cool rendition of the Christopher Cross classic "Sailing," and the guys "fly" — okay, in harnesses — over the audience. Whether by coincidence or fan conspiracy, Justin's the one most often left "dangling" over the audience when glitches in the contraptions stall it. Fans don't seem to mind a bit.

Solo Boy? Justin may be offered many opportunities for extra-band projects, but right now, just being part of 'N Sync is all he really wants. Which doesn't mean he's not totally behind his friends' side projects like Lance's "Free Lance Entertainment Company" (he manages up-and-coming acts), and Chris's in-development clothing line, FuManSkeeto.

15

CHAPTER THREE
JUST to the Rescue: What He'd Do

Here's one way to get to know Justin — find out how he'd handle a bunch of "emergency" situations. Check out the answers he gave in a recent interview.

1. EMERGENCY: A cat's stuck up in a tree.
JUSTIN'S SOLUTION: Get a ladder and climb up the tree. If you can't get the kitty down, call the fire department.

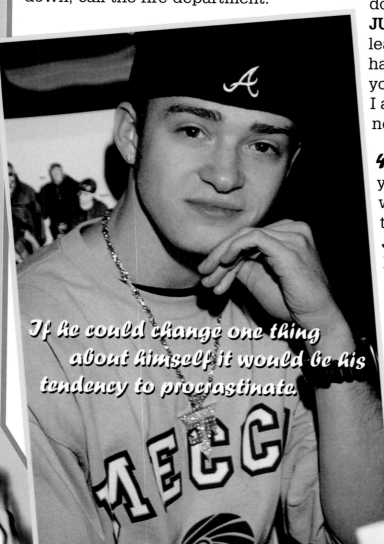

If he could change one thing about himself it would be his tendency to procrastinate.

2. EMERGENCY: Your pants have ripped onstage.
JUSTIN'S SOLUTION: Incorporate it into the show as a goofy move — and then run offstage as quickly as possible and change in a flash!

3. EMERGENCY: You just scraped the car next to you in a parking lot and you don't know whom it belongs to.
JUSTIN'S SOLUTION: All you can do is leave a note apologizing — of course, you have to leave your name and number so you can exchange insurance information. I am a great driver and hopefully this will never really happen.

4. EMERGENCY: You just realized you put on one brown sock and one white sock and it's one minute till showtime!
JUSTIN'S SOLUTION: Just go for it and hope you create a new fashion statement . . . and that the other guys in the group don't tease you!

5. EMERGENCY: You made dates with two different girls for the same night by accident.
JUSTIN'S SOLUTION: This one can get you in serious trouble! This is where a little white lie comes in. Tell the second girl you made the date with that something else "came up" so that her feelings aren't hurt. Then ask her out for a different night.

6. EMERGENCY: You said something in an article that was taken out of context and now embarrasses you.

JUSTIN'S SOLUTION: No solution here. This is just part of being in the fame game. Just pray that you didn't make anyone mad.

7. EMERGENCY: You wake up in the morning before a photo session and your face is full of zits.

JUSTIN'S SOLUTION: Wash your face and then let your makeup person take care of it with some kind of cover cream. 'N Sync's makeup professional also has a great shiny nose remedy — she puts hair pomade on a sponge and blots our honkers.

Guitar legend Jimi Hendrix is one of Justin's musical idols.

8. EMERGENCY: You have cooked dinner for a date but notice there is now a fly on the fettucini after you have put it in a serving dish.

JUSTIN'S SOLUTION: Someone else would throw the pasta away and send out for something. I, on the other hand, would just take out the fly and serve the food anyway. (Laughs.)

Sleep is what he misses most when the band's on tour. "We are always so hyped up after a show that it's hard to sleep," he told *Teen Girl Power* magazine. "Good thing I'm young or I wouldn't be able to get by on this little sleep. [But] it's hard for me to relax after a show, because I am so excited. Each show is a new success for us."

17

Justin

18

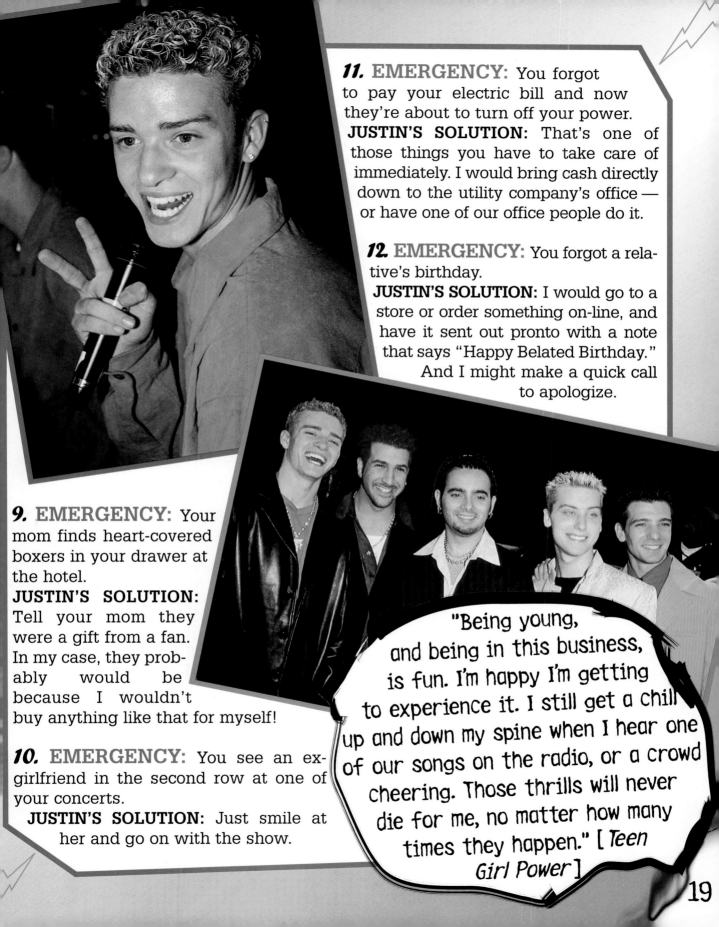

11. EMERGENCY: You forgot to pay your electric bill and now they're about to turn off your power.
JUSTIN'S SOLUTION: That's one of those things you have to take care of immediately. I would bring cash directly down to the utility company's office — or have one of our office people do it.

12. EMERGENCY: You forgot a relative's birthday.
JUSTIN'S SOLUTION: I would go to a store or order something on-line, and have it sent out pronto with a note that says "Happy Belated Birthday." And I might make a quick call to apologize.

9. EMERGENCY: Your mom finds heart-covered boxers in your drawer at the hotel.
JUSTIN'S SOLUTION: Tell your mom they were a gift from a fan. In my case, they probably would be because I wouldn't buy anything like that for myself!

10. EMERGENCY: You see an ex-girlfriend in the second row at one of your concerts.
JUSTIN'S SOLUTION: Just smile at her and go on with the show.

"Being young, and being in this business, is fun. I'm happy I'm getting to experience it. I still get a chill up and down my spine when I hear one of our songs on the radio, or a crowd cheering. Those thrills will never die for me, no matter how many times they happen." [*Teen Girl Power*]

19

CHAPTER FOUR
JUST the Real Deal: What He's Like Offstage

Want to get a glimpse into the real, offstage Justin Timberlake? Check it out.

He's Shy: Once Justin gets to know someone, he's totally talkative and out there, but he tends to step back a bit with people he hasn't met before. That's him being shy, not aloof. "The biggest misconception people have about me is that I'm into myself, or I'm stuck-up," he told a journalist, expaining of his natural reticence.

He's in the Phone Zone: When it comes to keeping in touch with those he loves, give Justin a cell phone over an e-mail account any day. As he told *Teen Girl Power* magazine, "I have a huge cell phone bill, but there are only a few people I really keep in touch with — basically family members and two or three close friends from back home." He doesn't often have a huge block of time just to sit and make calls, so he just presses "talk" whenever he can — sometimes the convos only last a few minutes, but at least, says Justin, "My friends and family always know I'm thinking of them."

He's Sports Boy: Hoops — there it is: Justin loves basketball and plays whenever

Justin's famous for his sneaker collection. At last count, he had over 70 pair. He told *SuperTeen* magazine, "I don't go out on the road with a lot of them, but I do take a separate bag for [new] sneakers. I get a duffel bag and fold it up and fill it up as I go!"

Tearin' it up onstage! The band is as famous for their out-there outfits as they are for their music.

just like them. . . . We do things just like them. . . . We like to go to the movies just like them. I find it funny that they get into us as much as they do, but I also find it flattering that they would take the time out to get into our music."

While Justin doesn't mind the attention that comes his way, he's always the first to remind people that he's only one-fifth of a band, and never would have become this popular without JC, Chris, Lance, and Joey.

He's Romantic: "I am a hopeless romantic," he confessed during a Yahoo! on-line chat. Once, for Valentine's Day, he surprised his date by cooking a pasta dinner and setting up a picnic, blanket and all, on her living room floor.

and wherever he can. Ever since I was a kid, if I wasn't singing, was playing basketball," he told *Teen* magazine. Michael Jordan is his all-time sports hero and his fantasy career goal is o walk (tall!) in Michael's footsteps. He's lso into in-line skating. "The rest of the group calls me Sporty Sync," he dished.

He's Spiritual: Though he'd never try to nfluence others, Justin is very open about his beliefs. "I consider myself blessed," he old a teen magazine. "I'm a very spiritual person."

He's Humble: In an AOL chat, he revealed, "It's funny that people actually ask me for autographs. The main thing I want our fans to [know] is that we are normal,

Crooning a love song: it's from the heart.

21

Wearing a cast on one hand (it was a broken thumb) and a puppet on the other, Justin is—hands down—the fan favorite.

He's a Homeboy: In spite of his mega-success, or maybe in a way because of it, when Justin's off the road, he heads not to his Orlando digs, but back to his real hometown. That's Memphis, Tennessee, a city he describes as "not too big, not too small, just homey," adding, "Like Dorothy said in *The Wizard of Oz*, there's no place like home." Of course, what's most meaningful to Justin are the people waiting for him there. That would be his mom Lynn and step-dad Paul, a banker. Also residing nearby, his dad Randy, stepmom Lisa, and little brothers Jonathan and Steven. Justin's grandparents are there, too, and he has close connections with them. "My granny cooked for me my whole life," he related, concluding, "I'm very Memphis, through and through!"

He's a Family Man: "I miss my family very, very much when I'm on the road," Justin revealed in an on-line interview. "[But] I talk to my mother every day. I think I have become closer to my family [now that] I don't

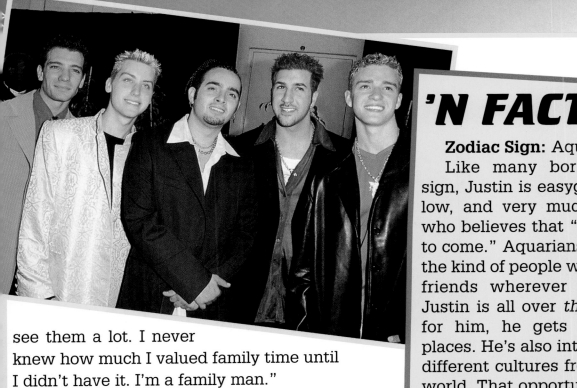

'N FACT!

Zodiac Sign: Aquarius

Like many born under that sign, Justin is easygoing and mellow, and very much an optimist who believes that "the best is yet to come." Aquarians are generally the kind of people who try to make friends wherever they go, and Justin is all over *that* trait. Lucky for him, he gets to go lots of places. He's also into checking out different cultures from around the world. That opportunity has led to his take on life: "People all over are looking for the same things — to be happy and to be loved."

see them a lot. I never knew how much I valued family time until I didn't have it. I'm a family man."

He Believes in Destiny: In a revealing on-line chat he said, "I don't think I was made to be normal. I think everybody has a destiny and I think this is mine."

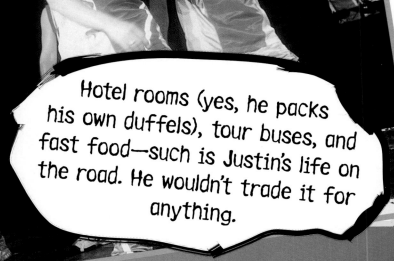

Hotel rooms (yes, he packs his own duffels), tour buses, and fast food—such is Justin's life on the road. He wouldn't trade it for anything.

Justin Timberlake

CHAPTER FIVE
JUST for You: The Love Connection

Justin is all over being in love — the concept of love, that is. He believes that each person not only *has* a soul mate, but *deserves* to find that person. Unlike lots of guys his age, he's not into dating many different girls at once, but feels best making a commitment. "I believe in relationships being long term, and I don't [go into] anything as just a fling," he told a reporter recently.

The huge downside to being in 'N Sync is that he doesn't have lots of time to find Ms. Right, and certainly not to nurture a relationship. He's always on the go. Even if the band isn't traveling, there are new songs to choose, tracks to record, choreography to practice, TV appearances to make, interviews and photo sessions to do.

He confided to *Teen Girl Power* magazine, "I meet lots of nice girls who seem really fun to be with and who I think are really beautiful, inside and out. But every time, no matter how special the girl is, things fizzle out. I can do my best and call every day and

If he had to choose one thing . . . among love, money or fame — it would be . . . love!

still, my career ends up being my priority. I have no choice. This is an all-encompassing thing. Very few people get to make a living at something they love to do, and even fewer people get to be stars. I count my blessings every day."

All this notwithstanding, he has had some experiences with girls.

First Sight: He believes it's possible to fall in love at first sight. "I believe in chemistry," he avowed during an AOL chat, "and I believe in certain feelings that you immediately develop when you meet someone that you think you can make a companion."

First Love: "The producers of *The New Mickey Mouse Club* gave a huge party, and I met a viewer who had won an invitation. We got on right from the start. I was head over heels in love. She was my first [big] love. We dated for nine months. But at the end of 1995, it was over. I had made a terrible discovery — she cheated on me with someone else. That's when my world ended. You cannot imagine how hurt and disillusioned I felt. I never want to be humiliated again. . . . I tried to forgive her. But she didn't want me anymore and she broke up with me. It took me six months to get over it." [*Joepie* magazine]

First Kiss: "It was when I was

> He is totally romantic, and proud of it.

ten years old. I was in the sixth grade and my girlfriend was in the eighth grade! [But] I was thirteen when I had my first real kiss."

First Date: When Justin was young, the first time he went out with a girl, he took her to the movies. These days, he'd probably do something a bit more daring — like skydiving! "Anything spur of the moment," he described to a reporter. "But not only wild

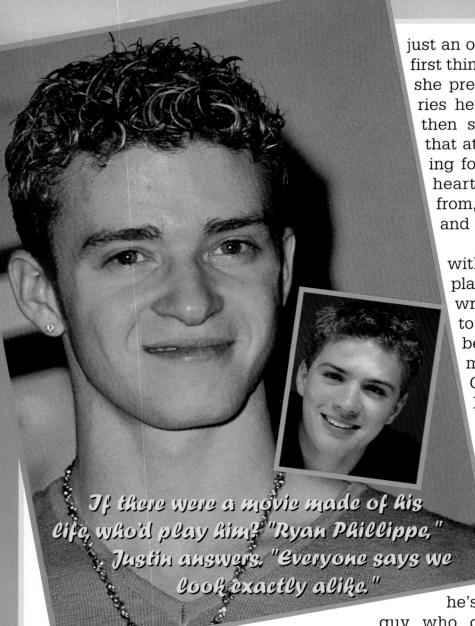

If there were a movie made of his life, who'd play him? "Ryan Phillippe," Justin answers. "Everyone says we look exactly alike."

just an overall picture. The first thing I notice is the way she presents herself and carries herself. If she's confident, then she's true to herself, and that attracts me to a girl. I'm looking for somebody with a sensitive heart, somebody I could learn from, that would complement me and help me grow as a person."

First Song: "If I was in love with somebody and wanted to play her a song, I'd probably write her a song, but if I wanted to play a song that's already been written, I could think of a million Stevie Wonder songs. Or there's this one song on Brian McKnight's first album called "Never Felt This Way" and it just, I don't know, it's the most direct way to say how you've never felt about someone before." [An AOL interview]

First With Fans: That fans rate Justin number one is obvious — and he's a "right back atcha" kind of guy who completely appreciates the attention. "We try to be there for everybody," he told a British magazine. "If possible, we give out autographs. We don't like to be 'ghost artists,' who don't have contact with our fans." Even though some kids have gone too far, like hanging out in trees outside his house, still, he *gets* it. "I know how these fans feel and I appreciate their enthusiasm."

First in His Heart? The talk about Justin's relationship with teen star Britney Spears started as a whisper,

things like skydiving. A quiet dinner, a good conversation is cool with me. Then I can get to know the girl."

First Rate: "Pretty is cool, but it's not really about looks for me. It's more about personality. I like a girl who's humble and sensitive," he told *Bop* magazine, adding, "She definitely has to have a sense of humor, and she has to be intelligent. I want to be able to talk to her. I guess I want

Fan appreciation sometimes comes in the form of stuffed animals that get tossed onto the stage. "We try to give some of them away to homeless shelters," Justin described in a Yahoo! chat.

but soon escalated into shouts around the world. In fact, it was the British press where "news" first broke about Justin and Britney being more than the Mickey Mouse Club "childhood" chums they said they were.

Denials from the pair were fast, furious, and consistent. Justin most always sticks to his "I'm single, available, and on the market" response when asked about his status. In a Yahoo! interview, he elaborated, "The rumors are not the truth. Britney is a very good friend of mine and we did do *Mickey Mouse Club* together. And I see her, but we're not dating. I consider her my little sister."

In an AOL chat, Britney talked about her relationship to all the 'N Sync-ers: "We are like brothers and sister. We were on the road together for three months [in 1998] and they were really nice guys and fun to be around."

When the rumor was raised by reporters during 'N Sync's appearance at the Virgin Megastore in New York City, Joey joked, *"I'm* actually dating

Justin on friends: "When someone is your true friend, [he or she] treats you the same way, no matter where you are in your life at that time." [Teen Girl Power]

29

Britney. We've been together for about seven years."

Lance added, *"I'm dating Britney and two of her dancers."*

Then came the media gossip item that Britney missed an autograph-signing gig back in September at Filene's department store because she'd rushed off with Justin to 'N Sync gigs in Mississippi and Tennessee, and didn't make it back on time. Neither she nor Justin has exactly copped to that one, but neither has exactly denied it, either.

So what *is* the deal between Brit and Justin? They're not saying any more than they already have, and until they do, no one can really be sure.

Future Love: Justin believes that he really won't be able to have a soul mate relationship for several more years. As he described to *Teen Girl Power,* "Someday all the frenzy and hype surrounding the group will die down. In some ways, that's good, because you get more of a private life and can take your time doing projects, and do what you have to in your personal life — spend time with your family. And at that point in my life, I will try to find my special girl

and have a relationship the right way — where we try to see each other as much as possible, and really get to know each other. And we'll do local things together like go to the beach or for ice cream, and all that kind of fun stuff.

"I also feel it's important for a guy to feel established in his life before he gets hitched. But I do feel 'established' now."

His all-time favorite songs?
"Every Stevie Wonder song," he typed in a Yahoo! chat. "Ribbon in the Sky,' 'My Cherie Amour,' —
I could go on!"

Justin believes in angels—in this shot, he looks like one.

'N FACT!

The Worst Date: Justin remembers this one girl who was majorly self-absorbed, and couldn't stop talking about herself. He admitted to *Teen Girl Power*, "I only ran into this girl once after our date, and she told me to call her, but I had no desire to. You can probably understand why . . . now I just want to be with someone who's got a good heart."

The band has one pre-show superstition. "We never go onstage until we've finished a hackey sack game. That's a must!" (Yahoo! chat)

31

CHAPTER SIX

JUST the Facts

'N Coming — 50 severely random bu[t] compulsively compelling (and cute) fac[t]toids about Justin Randall Timberlake!

1. He recently bought himself some wheels — a red Mercedes M-class!

2. He has an incredible fear of snakes — ditto, spiders and sharks.

3. He has a cat, Alley, and a dog, Ozzie.

4. His favorite drink is milk.

5. Best buds are: JC, Joey, Lance, and Chris.

6. His favorite cereal is Apple Jacks.

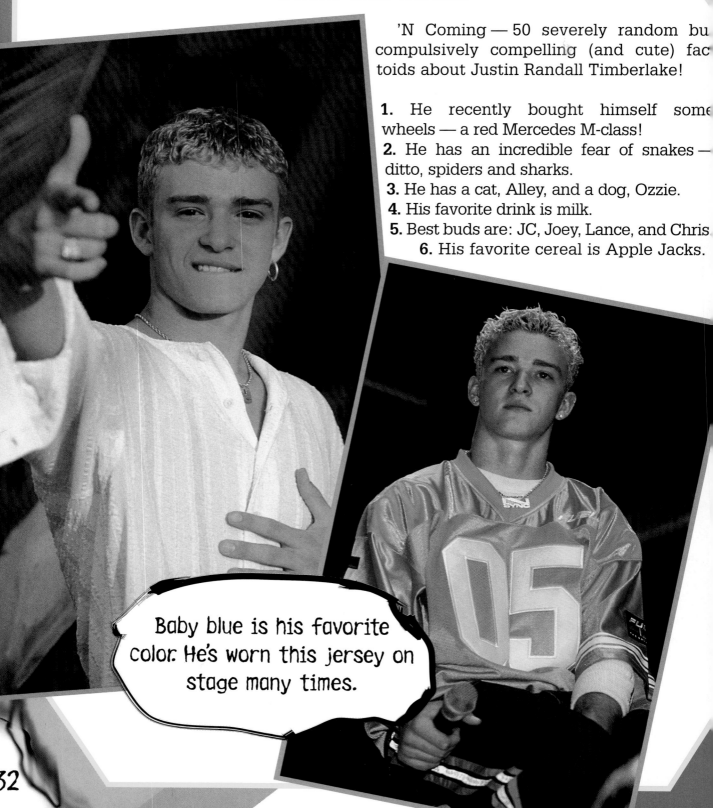

Baby blue is his favorite color. He's worn this jersey on stage many times.

Recording "Music of My Heart," with Gloria Estefan was a major thrill for Justin and the band—not to mention, a major hit

7. He has light brown hair that he bleaches blond.

8. Justin's favorite author is John Grisham and fave musician is Jimi Hendrix.

9. His favorite model is Tyra Banks.

10. Justin tried to iron his hair out once with a standard clothing iron and burned off the ends.

11. Justin has had problems recently with fans clipping off his curly locks — which makes him have to run out and get a trim to even out his hair!

12. Justin loves getting fan mail. You can write him at his official 'N Sync fan club address: 'N SYNC FAN CLUB, P.O. Box. 692109, Orlando, Florida 32869-2109 USA.

13. His favorite holiday is Christmas.

14. The thing he misses most on the road is SLEEP! He doesn't get enough.

15. He admits to being just a "little" superstitious.

16. He drinks lots of tea when his voice is getting raspy.

17. His favorite way to celebrate his birthday is with family and friends.

18. His biggest mistake ever was once telling a lie to his mom.

19. More than anything, he wants a "healthy life."

20. He wouldn't pierce his nose because it's a "dated look."

21. The most dangerous thing he has ever done is bungee jump!

22. The secret to his success is dedication and practice.

Concerts can cause a guy to sweat much, so Justin comes prepared: a towel and a bottle of water are always on hand.

23. He collects sneakers.
24. Justin just recently got an AOL account.
25. Musical inspirations include Brian McKnight and Take 6.
26. When asked what he'll be doing in 10 years he simply said, "I'll hopefully still be doing music."
27. He loves to wear the color baby blue — which he calls "North Carolina blue."
28. Justin says he knows an 'N Sync song is going to be a hit if it has a "good hook in it."

"I've never been in love," he admitted in a European magazine. "I've been infatuated, and had a few crushes. I won't run away when [the real thing] happens."

29. He is a strong believer in the phrase, "The show must go on!"

30. His greatest fear is "to die unloved," he admitted on the official 'N Sync Website.

1. Justin feels the group's best lyrics are in "God Must Have Spent a Little More Time on You."

2. He likes 'N Sync videos because they give the guys a chance to "show their personalities."

3. Justin says that being on tour is definitely one of the highlights of being in the music business.

4. Justin can play the piano as well as the guitar and he's got a private vocal coach.

35. The qualities he looks for in a girl are sensitivity and a good sense of humor.

36. He loved touring with Janet Jackson and says she was a big influence on him, along with her bro Michael!

37. The 'N Sync guys have a slew of nicknames for him including Curly, Shot, Bounce (because of his love for b-ball), The Baby, Mr. Smooth, Sporty Sync, and Curly Spice.

38. He likes to Rollerblade.

39. Justin adored doing a spring break shoot with MTV in Cancún,

Animal lover Justin posed with a leopard during an overseas photo shoot.

and hopes to get a real vacation there someday.

40. He lives in Orlando with his mom, and Chris and JC are frequent houseguests.

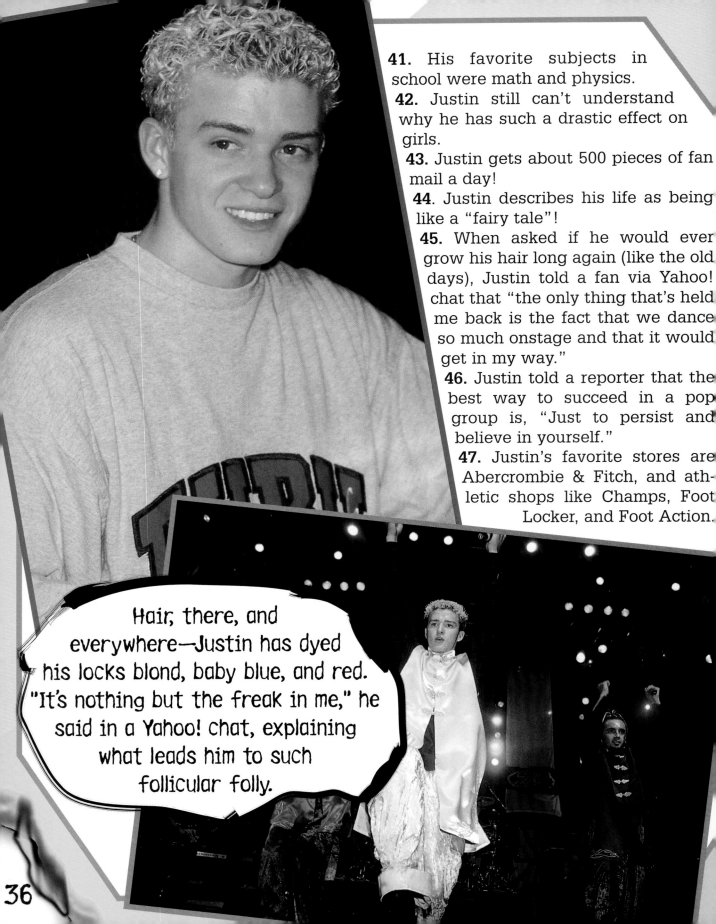

41. His favorite subjects in school were math and physics.

42. Justin still can't understand why he has such a drastic effect on girls.

43. Justin gets about 500 pieces of fan mail a day!

44. Justin describes his life as being like a "fairy tale"!

45. When asked if he would ever grow his hair long again (like the old days), Justin told a fan via Yahoo! chat that "the only thing that's held me back is the fact that we dance so much onstage and that it would get in my way."

46. Justin told a reporter that the best way to succeed in a pop group is, "Just to persist and believe in yourself."

47. Justin's favorite stores are Abercrombie & Fitch, and athletic shops like Champs, Foot Locker, and Foot Action.

Hair, there, and everywhere—Justin has dyed his locks blond, baby blue, and red. "It's nothing but the freak in me," he said in a Yahoo! chat, explaining what leads him to such follicular folly.

48. His favorite new cereal is Oreo O's.

49. His mom takes care of his car when he's away on tour.

50. Does Justin ever get air sickness? He said to *Teen Girl Power*, "Well, I've flown about five hundred to six hundred flights at this point, and so I have experienced it all — the very worst turbulence, the very worst airline food, the very longest flight delays, and the bumpiest landings. The worst feeling, though, is when a plane feels like it is 'falling.' Your stomach sinks!"

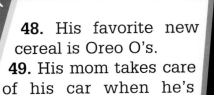

Titanic is one of Justin's all-time favorite movies— and yes, he admits, he cried.

Insecurity much? Only when people compliment him on his looks, he joked to *SuperTeen* magazine, adding, "I've never been too insecure. [It's more like] I blush when people compliment me. I kinda am bad with compliments. I kinda get embarrassed. I don't know what to say."

CHAPTER SEVEN
JUST in Concert
'N Sync 'N Concert Is 'N-Credible,
'N-Spiring, 'N-Tense! Here's Proof!

"We want to give the best live show," Justin told Teenbeat magazine. "We work really hard at it."

What goes through Justin's mind when he's onstage? "Quick — what's the next part?" he joked in a Yahoo! interview. "No, seriously, I love being onstage because the fans take the time to learn the words as soon as the song comes out. So it's cool to give them the microphone and let them sing it."

's been pointed out to Justin that onstage he holds the microphone right up against his lips. "That's where it's most comfortable for me to sing," he related in a Yahoo! chat.

How does Justin feel when the audience screams during an 'N Sync concert? "It pumps me up even more," he says. "We definitely dig it."

Justin's most embarrassing moments have come onstage. Once, his pants fell down (!!) and another time, he forgot the words to "I Want You Back." "We'd sung it so many times, that was pretty embarrassing!"

"I love touring because it gives everybody a chance to see you doing what you love to do, and it gives them a chance to relate to the songs and see the show."

41

"The coolest thing we do in concert is that we touch so many people with our music — that, and the positive outlook people get from it."

Justin's favorite onstage routine? The Jackson 5 medley they do, because "it's the most fun to dance to."

Is there a downside to being on the road and constantly touring? Justin misses three things: sleep, free time, and his family. But he wouldn't trade this life-style for anything. "My life is a fairy tale," he says.

CHAPTER EIGHT
JUST Amazing! A Mouse House of Stars!

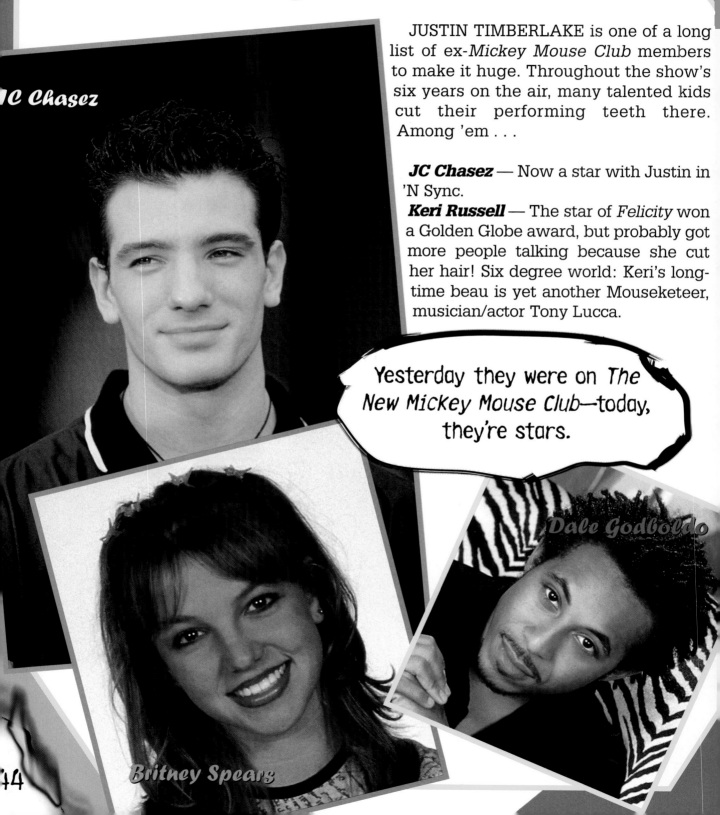

JC Chasez

JUSTIN TIMBERLAKE is one of a long list of ex-*Mickey Mouse Club* members to make it huge. Throughout the show's six years on the air, many talented kids cut their performing teeth there. Among 'em . . .

JC Chasez — Now a star with Justin in 'N Sync.

Keri Russell — The star of *Felicity* won a Golden Globe award, but probably got more people talking because she cut her hair! Six degree world: Keri's long-time beau is yet another Mouseketeer, musician/actor Tony Lucca.

Yesterday they were on *The New Mickey Mouse Club*—today, they're stars.

Dale Godboldo

Britney Spears

An 'N Sync concert is full of surprises—including these outrageous outfits.

Keri Russell

Britney Spears — Oh, bay-bay bay-bay, she sold more albums — six million and counting — than any other female teen star in history!

Christina Aguilera — She's a genie in a bottle all right, and those in the know say she's got major league pipes, which'll lead to a long career. She also beat out Puff Daddy for number one album when they were released the same week.

Dale Godboldo — The young actor now appears on the UPN TV show *Shasty McNasty*.

Christina Aguilera

CHAPTER NINE
JUST for the Record

An 'N Sync discography

'N Sync (First album — Europe)
1. "Tearin' Up My Heart" 2. "You Got It", 3. "Sailing" 4. "Crazy for You" 5. "Riddle" 6. "For the Girl Who Has Everything" 7. "I Need Love" 8. "Giddy Up" 9. "Here We Go" 10. "Best of My Life" 11. "More Than a Feeling" 12. "I Want You Back" 13. "Together Again" 14. "Forever Young"

'N Sync (First album — Canada)
1. "Tearin' Up My Heart" 2. "I Just Wanna Be With You" 3. "Here We Go" 4. "For the Girl Who Has Everything" 5. "God Must Have Spent a Little More Time on You" 6. "You Got It" 7. "I Need Love" 8. "I Want You Back" 9. "Everything I Own" 10. "I Drive Myself Crazy" 11. "Crazy for You" 12. "Sailing" 13. "Giddy Up"

The party was for *Teen People*'s anniversary, but the stars were 'N Sync!

Their first CD sold over seven million copies — no wonder they're on top!

'N Sync (First U.S. album — released March 1998)
1. "Tearin' Up My Heart" 2. "I Just Wanna Be With You" 3. "Here We Go" 4. "For the Girl Who Has Everything" 5. "God Must Have Spent a Little More Time on You" 6. "You Got It" 7. "I Need Love" 8. "I Want You Back" 9. "Everything I Own" 10. "I Drive Myself Crazy" 11. "Crazy for You" 12. "Sailing" 13. "Giddy Up"

Home for Christmas (released in November 1998)
1. "The First Noel" 2. "The Christmas Song" 3. "This Christmas" 4. "Holy Night" 5. "I Never Knew The Meaning of Christmas" 6. "Love's in Our Hearts on Christmas Day" 7. "Under My Tree" 8. "I Hear Angels"

9. "Will You Be Mine This Christmas?" 10. "It's Christmas" 11. "In Love on Christmas" 12. "Home for Christmas"

No Strings Attached (will be released in January 2000)
"Music of My Heart" was the first single.

U.S. SINGLES AND VIDEOS

"I Want You Back," "Tearin' Up My Heart" (radio track only), "God Must Have Spent a Little More Time on You," "I Drive Myself Crazy" (radio track only), "Music of My Heart"

SOUNDTRACKS

"Giddy Up" appears on the *Music from Sabrina the Teenage Witch* soundtrack.

CHAPTER TEN
JUST Look Ahead!

This year, Justin turns 19. His last year of being a teenager is already jam-packed with exciting things to come. There is new music and videos to make, new concerts to give, maybe a slew of new relationships as well.

On the music front: Justin's all over 'N Sync's new album, *No Strings Attached.* He agrees with what JC said in *Entertainment Weekly.* "This time the band took more creative control of the tracks." Fans will find a "more aggressive . . . style" under the jewel case.

On the acting front: Justin will co-star in the ABC-TV movie, *Cover Girls,* which airs February 13. He plays the boyfriend of a supermodel.

On the personal front: One of Justin's dreams is to have a home of his own. The big question is where? "I've been to so many places and said, 'I want to move here!' he told *Bop* magazine. "As of now, I really don't know. I really like Miami, Florida. The beach is great, [but] the mountains are great, too."

More plans: He also intends to take his education to the next level by enrolling in college one day.

Giving something back — especially to the people closest to his heart — is perhaps the most important of Justin's personal goals. His parents would be first on that list. "I told my parents, if we get lucky with this music career, I want to buy you guys a house, or build you a house wherever you want it."

And this one too: "When I'm older, I want to be able to look over my shoulder and say with pride that I've done many things in my life."

That's a goal Justin Randall Timberlake is well on his way to meeting.

The best advice he ever got? "Always try to do your best and never give up, no matter what happens." Those words of wisdom came courtesy of Mom.

The In My World Series

I live in a city

Bobbie Kalman
Susan Hughes

Toronto New York Crabtree Publishing Company

S0-DVF-108

The In My World Series
Created by Bobbie Kalman

Writing team:
Bobbie Kalman
Susan Hughes

Editor-in-Chief:
Bobbie Kalman

Editors:
Susan Hughes
Lise Gunby

Cover and title page design:
Oksana Ruczenczyn, Leslie Smart and Associates

Design and mechanicals:
Catherine Johnston
Nancy Cook

Illustrations:
Title page by Karen Harrison
Pages 28-29 by Deborah Drew-Brook-Cormack
© Crabtree Publishing Company 1985, 1986
Pages 4-27, 30-31, and cover © Mitchell Beazley Publishers 1982

Cataloging in Publication Data

Kalman, Bobbie, 1947–
    I live in a city

(The In my world series)
ISBN 0-86505-070-8 (bound) –
ISBN 0-86505-092-9 (pbk.)

1. City and town life – Juvenile literature.
I. Hughes, Susan, 1960– II. Title. III. Series.

HT119.K34   1986   j307.7'6

**To Heather and Peter
in London**

350 Fifth Avenue
Suite 3308
New York, N.Y. 10118

102 Torbrick Road
Toronto, Ontario
Canada M4J 4Z5

Contents

4

This is my neighborhood

This is my street. I live in the apartment building right above the fruit and vegetable store. Can you see me on the balcony? I am watching the painter paint the trim on one of our windows.

I know *all* of the people who live in my building. I know *many* of the people who live and work on my street. I know *some* of the people in my neighborhood. There are many people in my city whom I do not know. There are more than a million people living here!

I like to ride my bicycle around my neighborhood. I can visit Mrs. Pronk at the ice-cream store. I can say hello to Mr. McVittie, our letter carrier. Everywhere I go, I see people I know.

I have just met my new neighbors. They used to live on the other side of the city. They moved to our apartment building because their old apartment was too small for them!

I like this neighborhood. It is always changing. People move out and people move in. New shops and restaurants open up. Another building is being added to my school. There is a new wading pool in our park. My neighborhood is getting better and better all the time!

Picture talk

Is your neighborhood like this one? How is it the same? How is it different?
Has your neighborhood changed? How?
Draw a picture of your neighborhood. Mark your home on it. Show your favorite places.

Our community project

Today's the day! We have a lot of work ahead of us. Let's hurry to the community center.

Our community center is a special place for all the people in our community. A *community* is a neighborhood. It is both an area and the group of people who live together in it.

Our community center has ping-pong tables and a small library. It has board games and paint sets. There is always something interesting going on at the center. There are always friends to play with.

We take care of our community center together. Today we are building a swimming pool behind the center. We raised money by having bake sales, auctions, parties, and garage sales. Nat's father helped us to buy the materials we needed. Sarah's mother helped us with the plans for the pool.

My friends and I are digging the hole where the pool will go. It is hard work. Paul and Nat are prying a huge rock loose. I'm helping Lucinda to dig. Even my little sister Clea is working hard. She is filling her pail with small rocks.

We are all looking forward to our new pool. It will make the community center even more fun!

Picture talk
How are the people in this community cooperating?
How will these people feel when the job is done?
Why is it fun to work on a project with friends?

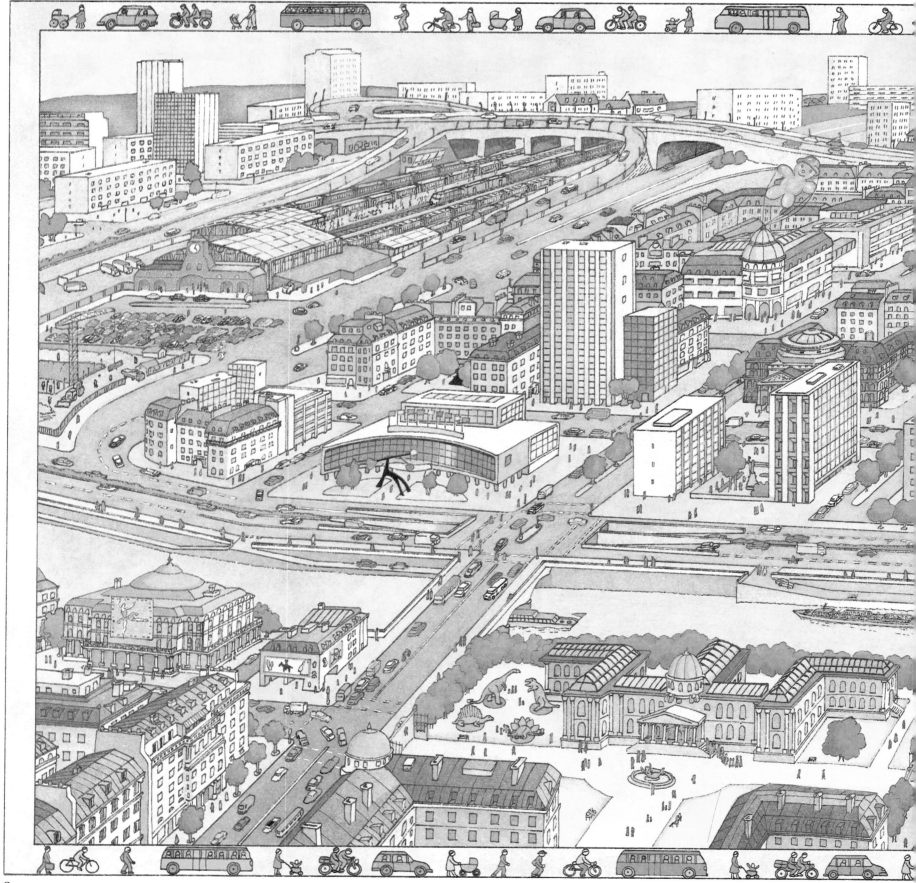

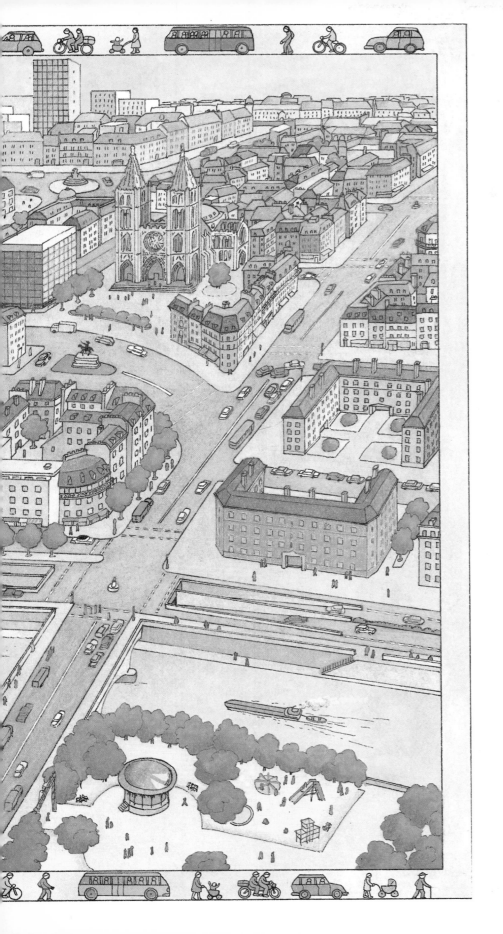

A city is a big community

Our city has churches and schools. It has factories, museums, theaters, a zoo, an amusement park, and a sports stadium. All these things could never fit into one small community!

There are many small communities in a city. Each of these communities is different. My community has a hospital. Another community near ours has a sports stadium. One community in our city even has a beach!

People in one community may use the services, parks, and buildings of another community. When people of different communities share what they have, the city becomes one big community!

People in a city elect a city government. They pay taxes to the government. The government uses the money to help run the city. The government uses the money to build streets and roads. It pays for the police and fire departments and for the subways and buses. It pays for schools and teachers. These are all *services* that help everyone who lives in the city.

Picture talk

What are some other city services?
Can you see the cathedral and the dinosaur exhibit?
Which is the art gallery? How can you tell?
Which is the train station?
Point to some apartment buildings. Would you like to live in this neighborhood? Why? Why not?

Rules and laws

A city is made up of thousands of people. When there are many people living in one place, they must cooperate. When you play a game, you agree on its *rules*. People who live together also have to agree on certain rules. Rules help people to get along with one another.

We have many traffic rules to keep us safe in the streets. These are some of them. Always cross the road at an intersection or crosswalk. Never cross the road from between parked cars. Never chase a ball that has rolled into the street.

Important rules are often made into *laws* by the government. One law is that no one can drive without a license. Traffic laws help to prevent people from being hurt. There are other kinds of laws, too. There are laws about marriage and laws about voting. There are laws about schools, businesses, buildings, and pets!

There are many people in a city who help to make laws work. Lawyers help people to understand the laws. Police officers help to protect people from those who break the laws. They also find the people who they suspect have broken the laws. If people do not obey laws, they are often punished. Judges help decide if people have broken the laws. They decide how people should be punished.

Picture talk

Which people in this picture are following the rules of the road?

Write down all the traffic rules you know.

What rules do you follow at school?

Travel in our city

Down to the railroad station to wait.
At 11:20, we go to the gate,
And here comes the train with a chug
    and choo-choo.
Off steps Grandma and Grandpa too!

They've traveled three hours from their
    small town.
They've crossed two rivers, gone uphill
    and down.
They've come all this way just to see me,
My parents, brother Paul, and our
    spotted dog, Flea!

Down to the subway! We'll all take a ride
From one end of the city to the other side.
We'll hop on a bus all the way to the zoo.
We'll look at the sights, some old and
    some new.

Now our grandparents must go, but not
    on the train.
They will visit my cousins and
    their city—by plane!
Out at the airport we'll say good-bye.
With a wave and a smile, away they will fly!

Picture talk

What kind of transportation did the grandparents use to travel to the city? in the city?
to leave the city?
Would you find all these kinds of transportation
in a town? Which ones would you find?
Why does a city need many kinds of
transportation?

Tall buildings

Many people live in this city. More people are moving in all the time. This city is growing and changing.

Why do cities have tall buildings? A tall building and a short building can take up the same amount of ground space. Many more people can live or work in a tall building than in a short building. A growing city needs many tall buildings for its *residents*. A resident is someone who lives or *resides* in a city.

Some new high-rise apartment buildings are being built in this neighborhood. The construction crew is working hard. The bulldozers have made the ground flat. Do you see the cranes? One is taking cement from the cement mixer. It is lifting the cement in a yellow bucket to the top of the building. Another crane is taking heavy steel girders from a truck. Can you see a third crane?

The engineer is checking the plans with the construction foremen. She must make sure that the plans are being followed exactly. The buildings must be made very strong so that people can live safely in them.

Picture talk
How can you tell this is a city?
How tall do you think this apartment building will be?
How many people do you think will live here?
How is living in an apartment different from living in a house? How is it the same?

15

I broke my arm today

My name is Lori. I was born in a hospital. Today I am at a hospital again. My friends and I were racing, and I fell. I broke my arm. An ambulance brought me to the emergency room. Doctor Alice put my arm in a cast. It did not hurt too much. Now Dad is taking me home.

Some of the children in this hospital have had accidents. Some of them are sick. The people who work here try to help them get better. Everyone here is really friendly. And there are lots of friends and toys to play with.

Dad says this hospital is one of the best hospitals in the country. It is just for children. It has special medical equipment. The doctors are all very good at caring for children. Some of the children who live in towns and villages nearby come to this hospital when they are very sick or need extra care.

I am glad we have such a good hospital in our city. It is nice to know that someone can patch me up when I get hurt!

Picture talk

How do doctors and nurses help the people in a community? Who are the other helpers in your community?

Name the community helpers who give the following services: mail delivery, protection, putting out fires, teaching children.

Would you like to be one of these helpers? Explain.

Shopping in the city

People need and want many things. They need food and clothing. They want furniture, clocks, toys, and books. They want television sets, dishes, carpets, and rakes.

Stores sell people these *goods*. Goods are things that are made to be sold. Producers are people who make or grow the goods. They sell the goods to *wholesalers*, who then sell them in large amounts to the stores. Stores sell the goods to *consumers*. Consumers are the people who use these goods or products.

Cities have many stores. Some stores sell records and others sell sporting goods. Some sell jewelry while still others sell shoes. Many cities also have *department stores*, such as the one in this picture. Department stores sell many different kinds of goods all in one store. Instead of going from shop to shop, people can try to get everything they want in one department store.

Different stores may sell the same product for different prices. Careful shoppers compare the prices of products. They buy the product they want at the lowest price they can find. Some stores have special sales. They sell goods at very low bargain prices.

Picture talk

What different goods can you see for sale in this department store?
What would you buy at this store?
Are you a producer or a consumer? Explain.

Our city is a port

Our city is a *port*. A port is a city with a harbor. Ships come here from all over the world. They bring products from other countries. Some of these products are sold in our shops. Some of them are transported by truck or train to other towns or cities. Ships also take products from this city to other countries.

Our city has factories which *manufacture* or make many products. Can you see some of the factories? My mother and father work at a huge car factory. Another factory nearby makes tractors. Some of the cars and tractors are sold in this city. Some of them are shipped to other cities and countries. Can you see the tractors being lifted onto the ship?

When people from this city sell products to other cities or countries, they receive money or other goods in return. This is called *trade*. When there is a lot of trade, the people selling the products earn a lot of money. They spend this money in the city. When many people earn and spend money in a city, and trade and business grow, the city grows too. Our city is a growing port city!

Picture talk

What is the ship carrying in boxes?
Where might the trucks be taking the fruit?
Where might the other ships be going?
Is your community a port community? What products are manufactured in your community? Find out where ten products in your home were made. Which ones were transported by ship?

Places of worship

People follow many religions. They build places where they can pray and worship. These places of worship are called by different names. Some people worship in churches, some in temples, some in mosques, and some in synagogues. There are many places of worship in a city.

A visit to a cathedral

Paulo and his father are on vacation. They have come to visit our city. They have come to see our beautiful cathedral.

A *cathedral* is a very big church. Most cathedrals were built a long time ago. Our cathedral is very old. It is made of stone. The stone is carved in interesting patterns and shapes. There are many beautiful stained-glass windows. When the light shines in, the colors in the windows glow.

Paulo is reading a brochure which tells the history of the cathedral. The cathedral was built when the city was small. The city has grown a lot over the years. Many new buildings have been added. The cathedral is one of the oldest buildings in our city.

Picture talk

Is this cathedral an important part of this city? Why?
Do you go to a place of worship? What is it called?
Are there any old buildings in your community? What are they?
What interesting places might tourists want to visit in your city?

23

24

Space Village

Many tourists visit our city. They say they come to see our buildings and enjoy our theaters and museums, but I know why they really come. They come to see Space Village.

Space Village was built a few years ago. I don't know how we ever got along without it! I go there at least once a month. Everything in Space Village belongs to the future. There is a supersonic Flying Saucer. It is made of rubber on the outside. The inside is filled with thousands of tiny plastic balls. You can crawl in headfirst and cover yourself in balls until only your face shows!

There are space cones, space mushrooms, space caves, and space monsters. My favorite ride is the Space Flume. It starts out near the Flying Saucer, travels between Astro Monster's legs, and through Lunar Boulder. Then it speeds around Future City and drops suddenly down, down, down, until — SPLASH! It comes to a halt in the Cosmic Puddle.

Space Village has great rides, strange music, and weird-looking food. The people who work at Space Village look like robots and space creatures. I wonder if our city will look like Space Village in the future. It sure would be fun!

Picture talk
Name the rides and creatures in Space Village.
What might homes of the future look like?
How would a future city differ from your city?

My multicultural city

Our city is really exciting. People from many different countries live here. They have brought their cultures to this city. Do you know what *culture* means? Culture is the way a group of people lives. Culture is the kind of food people eat, the clothes they wear, the music they listen to, and the ways they celebrate. Our city is *multicultural*. Multicultural means "made up of many cultures."

My father was born in Portugal. My mother was born in Canada. I was born in the United States. We live in a community where many people are Chinese. Our family celebrates the holidays of all these cultures. I guess that makes me multicultural, too!

Chinese New Year is one of my favorite holidays. It comes at a different time each year, but it is always between January 20 and February 20. The best part of Chinese New Year is the dragon dance. People from all over the city come to our neighborhood to see the dance.

The dragon is a huge costume worn by many people. Can you see their feet? The body is made of colorful cloth. The dragon's head moves up and down and from side to side. Musicians play drums and gongs. People clap, whistle, and cheer. They yell, "Happy New Year!"

Picture talk
What do you think is written on these banners and signs?
How do you celebrate New Year? Ask five of your friends how they celebrate.

27

What is a city?

A city is a big community made up of many small communities. Cities offer goods, shelter, and many services to their residents.

Below is a list of many of the things that make up a city. Match these things to the numbered pictures. Some of the pictures will have more than one match. For example, a doctor would be matched with "jobs" as well as "people" and "services."

A. services
B. places of worship
C. communication
D. transportation
E. goods
F. people
G. shelter
H. culture
I. leadership
J. jobs
K. entertainment
L. education
M. protection
N. utilities

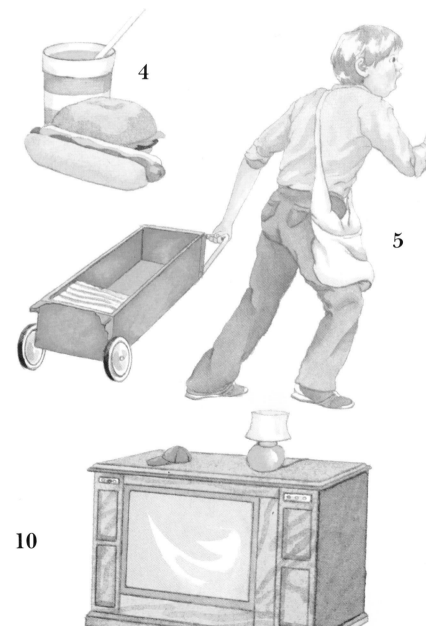

4

5

10

1

Answers:

1. A, D; 2. F, I, J; 3. A, D, J, L; 4. E; 5. C, F, J; 6. F; 7. H (Dinosaur skeletons are found in museums); 8. A, F, J, M; 9. A, F, J, M; 10. A, C, E, K, N; 11. G; 12. K; 13. B, H, L

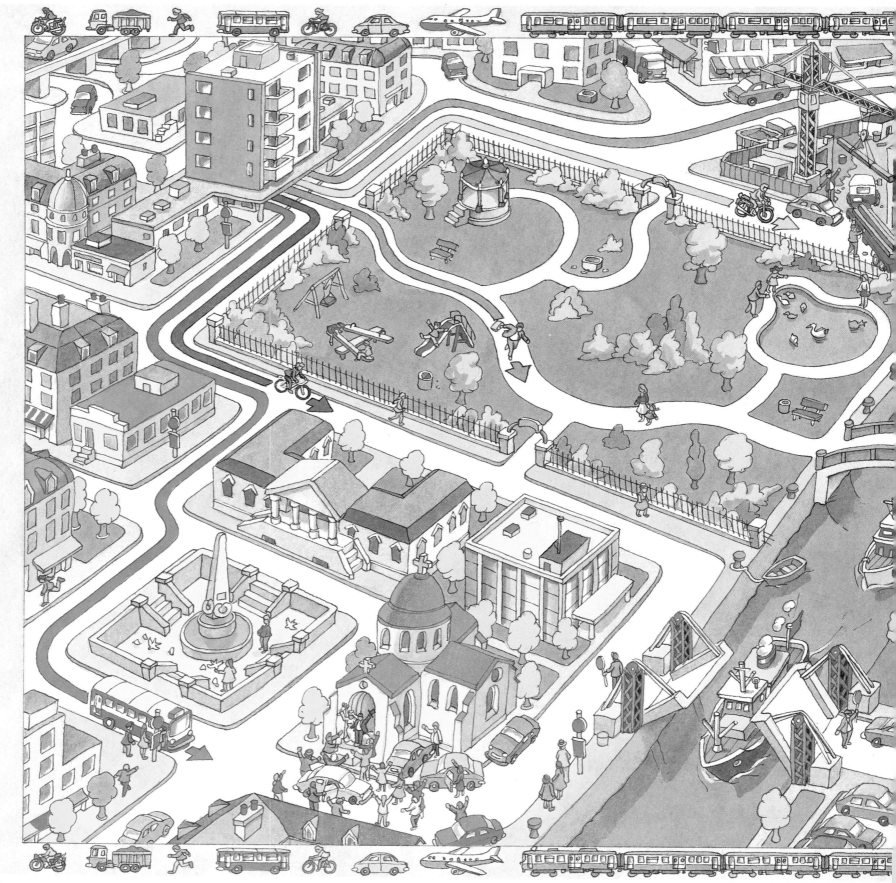

Try this...
Who will get there first?

Mr. Landis, Mrs. Porter, Mr. Hughes, Andrea Crabtree, and Jason Kudo all live in the same apartment building. Each of them is going to the train station. Can you find it in the picture?

Jason took the bus. Mr. Hughes drove his car. Andrea hopped on her bicycle. Mr. Landis ran out the front door. Mrs. Porter, wearing her bright-yellow helmet, roared out on her motorcycle.

Each of these neighbors is taking a different route. Each of them is traveling at a different speed. Follow their paths. Decide who will reach the train station first, second, third, fourth, and last. Give a reason for each of your choices.

Mystery location

Follow the clues and find the mystery location in the picture. You must solve each clue as you come to it or you might end up in the wrong place. Here are your clues:
1. Begin at the man who is riding a horse.
2. Cross some water and then pass a wheelbarrow.
3. Turn left at the first intersection and keep going until you see something round with seven poles.
4. Walk past an object that goes up and down. Exit through an archway.
5. Go left, then right, then right again. Arrive in time to say, "Congratulations!"
6. Point to the mystery location. What is it?

Answer: The church

City dictionary

bargain Something bought or offered for sale at a low price.

brochure A booklet or pamphlet.

cathedral A large or important church.

church A building for religious worship, usually Christian.

city A large, important center where many people live and work. A city provides its residents with shelter, goods, and services.

communication The exchange of ideas or information by such means as writing or speaking.

community Both an area and the group of people who live together in it.

department store A large store that sells many kinds of goods and is organized into departments according to the kinds of goods sold.

engineer A person who is trained to plan and build structures that require much scientific knowledge, such as roads, machinery, and canals.

factory A building or group of buildings where goods are made.

foreman A worker who is in charge of a group of workers.

girder A long steel or wooden beam used to support the framework of bridges, buildings, and other structures.

goods Things that are made to be bought and sold.

government A group of people who govern. To govern means to make and direct plans of action which will affect the people.

harbor A place or port where ships can be sheltered or anchored.

high-rise A tall building with many stories.

law A rule made by the government for its people.

lawyer A person who is trained to give advice about laws and to represent clients in court.

licence Legal permission to do or own something.

manufacture To make large quantities of products.

mosque A temple where Moslems worship.

multicultural Having many cultures.

neighborhood A small section or area of a town or city and the people who live there.

product Something that is made.

resident A person who lives in a certain place; not a visitor.

rule A direction that tells the correct way to do something or what may or may not be done.

service A way of providing help to the public, such as having a bus service.

synagogue A building or place used by Jews for religious instruction and worship.

tax A certain part of the money people earn which is paid to the government. The government uses this money to pay for services for the public.

temple A building for religious worship, such as a synagogue or a Hindu temple.

tourist A person traveling for pleasure.

trade The business of buying and selling.

transportation The act of carrying something from one place to another.

voting Making a choice in an election. People elect those who will be members of the government.

worship The honor and love given to God.

23456789   BP   Printed in Canada   43210987